For my agent, Becky Bagnell. Thank you for your wisdom,
support and friendship. You are awesome! - PB

For Natacha - MB

Bloomsbury Publishing,
London, New Delhi, New York and Sydney

First published in Great Britain in 2015
by Bloomsbury Publishing Plc
50 Bedford Square, London, WC1B 3DP

This paperback edition first published in 2015

A CIP catalogue record for this book
is available from the British Library

ISBN 978 1 4088 3903 4 (HB)
ISBN 978 1 4088 3904 1 (PB)
ISBN 978 1 4088 7126 3 (Reduced-size PB)
ISBN 978 1 4088 3902 7 (eBook)

Printed in China by Leo Paper Products, Heshan, Guangdong

13 5 7 9 10 8 6 4 2

All papers used by Bloomsbury Publishing are natural, recyclable products
made from wood grown in well-managed forests. The manufacturing processes
conform to the environmental regulations of the country of origin

www.bloomsbury.com

BLOOMSBURY is a registered trademark
of Bloomsbury Publishing Plc

Never Tickle a Tiger

Pamela Butchart

Illustrated by
Marc Boutavant

BLOOMSBURY

LONDON NEW DELHI NEW YORK SYDNEY

Izzy was forever **shuffling** and jiggling,
squirming and twitching,
wriggling and fiddling.

She just couldn't help it.

It happened at home . . .

"Izzy, **stop** playing with your peas!" said Dad.

At school . . .

"Izzy, **stop** painting your pigtails," said Miss Potterhurst.

At Grandma's . . .

"Izzy, **stop** knotting my knitting," said Grandma.

And as for at parties, well . . .

"Izzy, stop jiggling the jelly!" cried everyone.

No matter how hard she tried, Izzy just couldn't keep still.
"It's no good," she sighed. "I'm just a jiggler and that's that."

So when, one day, class 4B went on a trip to the zoo, it came as
no surprise to anyone that Izzy was wriggling, jiggling,
shuffling and fiddling as soon as they walked through the zoo gates.

"Stop stroking the snakes," called Miss Potterhurst.

"Don't excite the elephants."

"Forget about bothering the bears."

"Don't **mess** with the monkeys."

"Izzy, **stop** tapping the tortoises."

"**Stop** poking the peacock."

"And **never** ever tickle a tiger!"

At lunchtime, Izzy sat shuffling her sandwiches.

"It's so unfair," she said. "I'm **never** allowed to do anything.
And what's wrong with fidgeting anyway?"

Little did Izzy know that she was about to find out!

Whilst all the other children finished
their lunch,

Izzy fidgeted her feet,

bounced across the bench,

shimmied on to the floor,

wriggled under a bush,

skipped past the aviary
and danced along a path
all the way to . . .

the **tiger** enclosure!

who bit a bear . . . who walloped a walrus . . . who splashed a sloth . . . who punched a penguin . . .

"Raa-aa-ah!" roared the tiger. He threw his furry paws in the air ...
which broke a branch ... which startled a snake ...

"I wonder?" thought Izzy and, with that,
she reached out a feather
and tickle,
tickle,
tickled the tiger!

who rammed a rhino . . . who hit the hippo . . . who wibbled and wobbled and . . .

who kicked a croc . . . who snapped at a skunk . . . who ponged a panda . . .

. . . SPLAAAAASH!

The lion roared, the parrots squawked, the snakes hissed and the elephants trumpeted loudly. Miss Potterhurst squealed, the children giggled and the zookeeper came running.

It was pandemonium!
And it was all Izzy's fault. But then . . .

"STOP!" shouted Izzy at the top of her voice.
"Stop squealing, squawking,
splashing and flapping. Enough running,
roaming, ramming and bumping.
No more jiggling, wriggling,
shuffling and squirming!"

And guess what?
It worked! The zookeeper stopped running,
Miss Potterhurst stopped squealing,
the children stopped giggling
and all the animals went back to their homes.
And as for Izzy . . .

"You were right all along, Miss Potterhurst," she said.
"I'll never ever **tickle** a tiger again."

But . . .

Polar
Bear

What can be the harm of prodding
a polar bear? she thought.